Ultimate Science Lab

EXPERIMENTS with MOVEMENT

Anna Claybourne

Gareth Stevens
PUBLISHING

Please visit our website, www.garethstevens.com. For a free color catalog of all our high-quality books, call toll free 1-800-542-2595 or fax 1-877-542-2596.

Cataloging-in-Publication Data

Names: Claybourne, Anna.
Title: Experiments with movement / Anna Claybourne.
Description: New York : Gareth Stevens Publishing, 2019. | Series: Ultimate science lab | Includes glossary and index.
Identifiers: ISBN 9781538235423 (pbk.) | ISBN 9781538235447 (library bound) | ISBN 9781538235430 (6pack)
Subjects: LCSH: Motion--Experiments--Juvenile literature. | Motion--Juvenile literature.
Classification: LCC QC127.4 C5725 2019 | DDC 531'.11078--dc23

First Edition

Published in 2019 by
Gareth Stevens Publishing
111 East 14th Street, Suite 349
New York, NY 10003

Copyright © Arcturus Holdings Ltd, 2019

Author: Anna Claybourne
Science consultant: Thomas Canavan
Experiment illustrations: Jessica Secheret
Other illustrations: Richard Watson
Photos: Shutterstock
Design: Supriya Sahai, with Emma Randall
Editor: Joe Fullman, with Julia Adams

Printed in the United States of America

CPSIA compliance information: Batch #CW19GS: For further information contact Gareth Stevens, New York, New York at 1-800-542-2595.

CONTENTS

START EXPERIMENTING!

This book is packed with exciting experiments that go zoom, whoosh and fly, or are so incredible you won't believe your eyes! But there's nothing magical in these pages—it's all real-life amazing **SCIENCE**.

BE ECO-FRIENDLY!

First things first. As scientists, we aim to be as environmentally friendly as possible. Experiments require lots of different materials, including plastic ones, so we need to make sure we reuse and recycle as much as we can ...

★ Some experiments use plastic straws; rather than buying a large amount, ask in coffee shops or restaurants whether they can spare a few for your experiments.

★ Old cereal boxes are great for experiments that use cardboard.

★ Save old school worksheets and other paper you no longer need, to reuse for experiments.

WHAT YOU'LL NEED

You can do most of these experiments with everyday items you'll find around the house.

Some useful things to have handy are ...

* Paper and cardboard
* Pens and pencils
* String
* Glue
* Tape
* Straws (plastic ones are best)
* Plates, bowls, jugs, and plastic food containers
* Scissors
* Rubber bands
* Paper cups
* Balloons

STAY SAFE!

Experiments are fun, but some of them can be dangerous if they're not done carefully ... so don't forget these safety tips:

✴ You will need an adult to help with experiments that involve cooking and heating, matches and candles, and sharp cutting tools. Wherever an experiment has something like this in it, you'll see this sign to remind you:

⚠ ASK AN ADULT!

✴ Follow all the instructions carefully to make sure you use all the equipment and materials in a safe way.

✴ If an experiment requires you to stand on a chair, make sure you have someone to assist you. Check that the chair is placed in a stable position and ask the person helping you to hold the chair while you are using it.

✱ Stand back from anything that's moving fast, or that involves eruptions or explosions. And don't throw, shoot, or whirl things around unless you're completely sure there's no one nearby.

And remember...

Always do experiments somewhere that's easy to clean up, like a kitchen or bathroom—NOT on the fancy carpet! And make sure you do clean up after yourself. Some of these experiments are messy!

So, are you ready to see some science? Step this way …

SPEEDY EXPERIMENTS

The experiments in this book are all about making things move, which is an important part of science and technology. Understanding movement means we can make all kinds of vehicles, so that we can travel to school, the stores... or even into space!

HOW MOVEMENT WORKS
To make things go, something needs to pull them or push against them. In other words, you need a force. There are lots of types of forces you can use, and you'll meet several of them in this book.

ROCKET POWER: When gas rushes out of something, it pushes that thing the other way.

PADDLE POWER: A moving paddle pushes against water, making a boat move.

ELASTIC POWER: Energy stored in something springy or elastic can be turned into movement.

GRAVITY: This pulling force makes things fall downward or roll downhill.

ELECTRICITY: An electrical spark is a flow of high-speed particles.

The ball test

To start with, try this movement experiment in a safe open space outdoors. You'll need two balls—a large one, like a basketball, and a smaller one, like a tennis ball or a bouncy rubber ball.

Hold the balls up with the smaller ball sitting right on top of the larger one, then drop them together. What happens?

If it works, you'll see the big ball bounce back up a little way, and the small ball zoom up really high!

HOW DOES iT WORK?

Movement is a kind of energy. It you put more energy in, you'll get more movement out. When the big ball drops, it hits the ground and bounces back up. Right away it hits the small ball on top of it. Some of the movement energy from the big ball passes into the small ball. The small ball is lighter, so the extra energy makes it move much faster.

WATCH OUT!
Be careful when performing these high-speed experiments. Make sure you have plenty of space to work in, and stand well back from fast-moving objects.

BALLOON-POWERED CAR

Use the air shooting out of a balloon to drive a toy car forward. How fast can you make it go?

WHAT YOU'LL NEED:

* Strong, stiff cardboard
* Three straws
* Two wooden skewers
* Strong scissors
* Clear tape
* A marker
* A sharp pencil
* A balloon

! ASK AN ADULT!

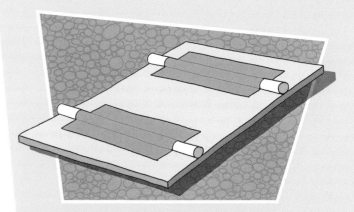

1. Cut a rectangle of cardboard the size of a small book. Cut two straws so they're the same width as (or just slightly longer than) the cardboard. Tape them to the cardboard.

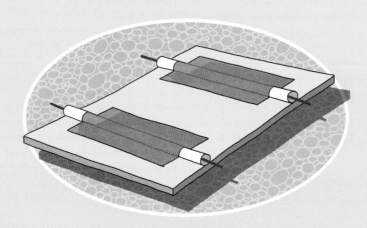

2. Ask an adult to use strong scissors to cut the wooden skewers so they are about 1 inch (2.5 cm) longer than the cut straws. Thread the skewers through the straws.

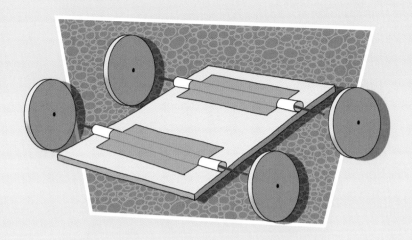

3. Draw around a round object onto some more cardboard to make four wheels, 3 inches (8 cm) across. Cut them out and ask an adult to make a small hole in the middle of each one, using the pencil. Push the wheels onto the ends of the skewers, and turn your car over.

4. Blow the balloon up to stretch it, then let the air out. Now cut off the thick part at the opening, and stick your third straw inside. Wrap the tape around them both to make a tight seal.

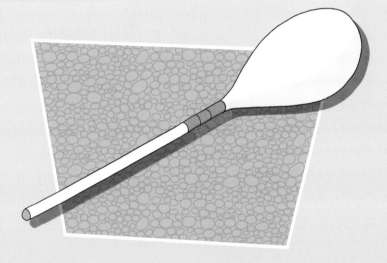

5. Tape part of the straw onto the top of your car, with the open end overlapping the end of the cardboard. The balloon should rest on top of the car. Blow into the straw to inflate the balloon, then put the car on the ground and let it go!

HOW DOES IT WORK?
Blowing up the balloon fills it with squeezed, pressurized air. When you let it go, the air shoots out of the straw. The moving air pushes back on the straw, and this pushes the car along.

FLYING MARBLES

If you wanted to jump over a big gap, you'd take a big run-up. Help these marbles do the same with a high-speed jump ramp.

WHAT YOU'LL NEED:

* Marbles
* A foam pipe insulation tube, from a hardware store
* Scissors
* Heavy-duty packing tape or duct tape
* Books
* Removable clear tape
* A plastic bowl or container

⚠ ASK AN ADULT!

1. Take your tube and ask an adult to cut it in half lengthways to make two half-tubes. Join the ends of the tubes together using heavy-duty tape, to make one super-long channel.

> If you have more tubes, you could make a really long channel. See if it's long enough to build a roller coaster with a loop-the-loop.

2. Use removable clear tape to fix one end of the ramp to a doorframe, and curve the lower end upward to make a ramp. Use a pile of books to support the ramp.

3. Hold a marble a little way up the slope, and let it go so that it rolls down. Try rolling the marble from higher up the slope, then try rolling it from the very top. What happens?

If you have them, experiment with different sizes of marble. Do bigger, heavier marbles roll faster or slower?

4. Put the plastic bowl near the end of the ramp, and try to roll marbles from the top so that they fly off the ramp and land in the bowl. It's not as easy as it looks!

HOW DOES IT WORK?

As a ball rolls down a slope, it starts off slowly. But as gravity keeps pulling on it, it picks up speed and goes faster and faster, or "accelerates." The higher up it starts, the faster it will go. Marbles that have picked up a lot of speed will fly off the end of the ramp and jump a big gap.

AIR-POWERED ROCKET

Fancy flying your very own spacecraft? Follow these steps to build your own rocket ship, which uses air pressure to shoot high in the air.

WHAT YOU'LL NEED:

* ★ An empty, clean, plastic detergent or drink bottle
* ★ A straw
* ★ Modeling clay or poster putty
* ★ Paper
* ★ Markers
* ★ Scissors
* ★ Clear tape

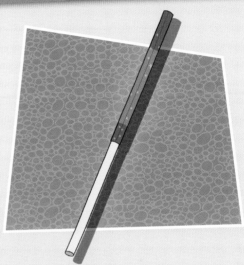

1. First, make your rocket. Cut a rectangle of paper about 2 x 3 inches (5 x 8 cm), and roll it around the straw. Tape it in place to make a tube. It should be a snug fit, but not too tight. The paper should be able to slide up and down the straw easily.

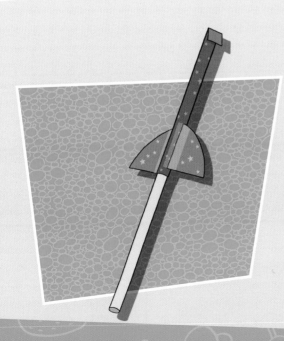

2. Fold over and flatten the end of the paper to make your rocket's nose. You can also add paper fins to its base to help it fly.

You could use more paper to draw a large, round moon to act as a target for your rocket. See if you can hit it right in the middle.

3. Roll a ball of modeling clay or poster putty slightly bigger than the neck of the bottle. Wrap it around the straw so that the end sticks out, making sure the straw is not squashed flat. Fit the ball and the straw tightly onto the bottle neck, like this.

4. Now squeeze the bottle hard and watch your rocket fly. How high can you make it go?

HOW DOES IT WORK?

The bottle rocket launcher is full of air. When you squeeze it suddenly, air is forced down the straw and pushes hard against the rocket on the end, firing it forward at high speed.

ANTIGRAVITY CUP

If you fill a cup with water and then turn it upside down, the water will fall out — won't it? Not if it's flying fast enough!

WHAT YOU'LL NEED:
* A disposable paper or plastic cup
* Strong string
* Strong clear tape or duct tape
* Pointy scissors
* Water
* Nerves of steel

⚠ ASK AN ADULT!

1. Ask an adult to make two holes in the cup, one on either side just below the rim, using the pointy scissors.

2. Cut a piece of string about 6 feet (2 m) long, and thread the ends through the holes. Tie each end on firmly, so that the string makes a long handle.

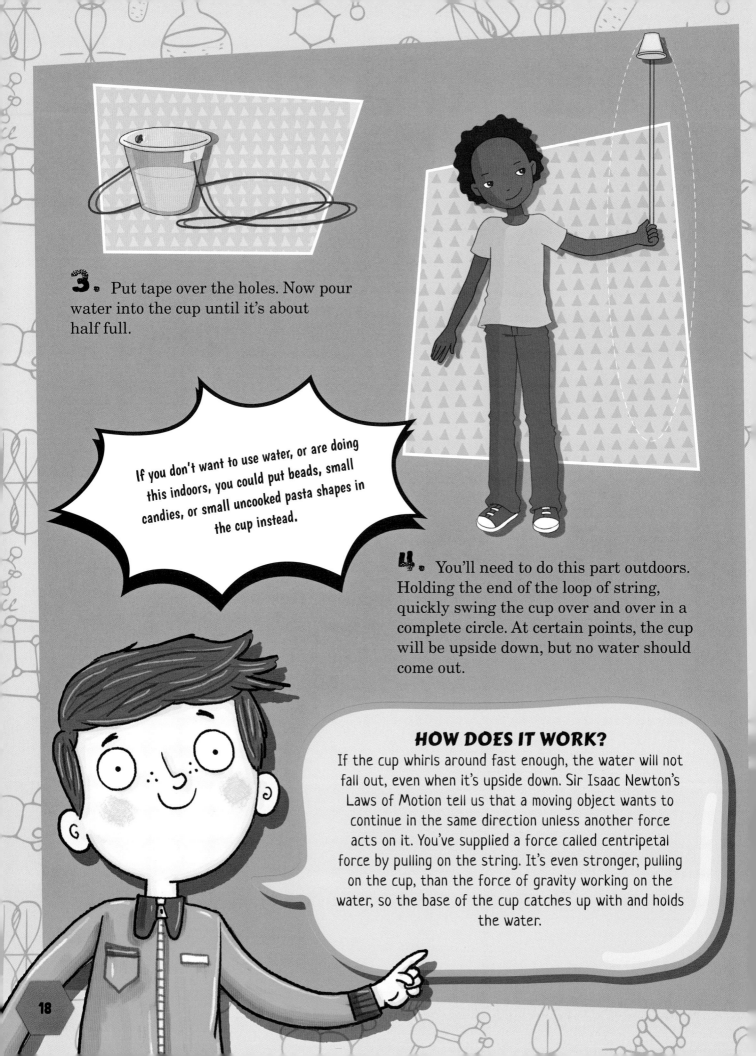

3. Put tape over the holes. Now pour water into the cup until it's about half full.

If you don't want to use water, or are doing this indoors, you could put beads, small candies, or small uncooked pasta shapes in the cup instead.

4. You'll need to do this part outdoors. Holding the end of the loop of string, quickly swing the cup over and over in a complete circle. At certain points, the cup will be upside down, but no water should come out.

HOW DOES IT WORK?

If the cup whirls around fast enough, the water will not fall out, even when it's upside down. Sir Isaac Newton's Laws of Motion tell us that a moving object wants to continue in the same direction unless another force acts on it. You've supplied a force called centripetal force by pulling on the string. It's even stronger, pulling on the cup, than the force of gravity working on the water, so the base of the cup catches up with and holds the water.

MAKE TINY LIGHTNING!

We're not joking — in this experiment you really can make a flash of lightning, just like the lightning you see in a thunderstorm. The only difference is it's really, really tiny! (And a lot safer.)

WHAT YOU'LL NEED:
* A balloon
* A metal spoon
* A completely dark room

1. First, get your room ready. Unless it has no windows, it will be easiest to make it really dark when it's also dark outside. Switch off the lights, any screens, and machines with LEDs.

2. Outside the room (so you can see what you're doing), blow up the balloon and tie it. Hold the spoon in one hand and the balloon in the other. Now rub the balloon on your hair, quite fast, for a long time—at least a minute.

Yes, you'll get super-messy hair. Sorry about that!

3. Keeping the balloon and the spoon apart, and not touching anything, go into the dark room (getting someone else to close the door for you).

HOW DOES IT WORK?

The rubbing makes tiny things called electrons come off your hair and onto the balloon. These extra electrons build up and give the balloon an electric charge, called static electricity. When the spoon comes near the balloon, the electrons jump across the gap as a spark of electricity.

4. Now hold the balloon up in front of you, and slowly move the spoon toward it. If you've rubbed the balloon enough, a mini lightning spark will zap across the gap!

SURFACE SPEED

You can't see it, but the surface of water has a strange "skin" on it that can make it behave in weird ways. It's called surface tension.

WHAT YOU'LL NEED:
* A large, shallow bowl or plate
* A pitcher
* Water
* Glitter or black pepper
* Dishwashing liquid
* Craft foam
* Scissors

1. Put the bowl on a flat surface and carefully fill it with water, using the pitcher. When the surface is calm and flat, gently sprinkle some glitter or pepper onto it. It should mostly stay on the surface.

2. Squeeze a little dishwashing liquid onto the tip of your finger. Then dip your finger into the water, right in the middle. What happens?

A tiny lizard, called a pygmy gecko, can use surface tension to walk on water.

21

3. Clean the plate or bowl and start again with fresh water. This time, cut a small surfboard shape out of the craft foam, like this. Make a little notch in the back. Put the surfboard in the water. It should float motionless on the surface.

As well as pepper or glitter, surface tension can hold up larger objects, such as metal pins and paper clips. Try it! Then try adding some dishwashing liquid to the water.

4. Now take the surfboard out of the water, and use your finger to put a blob of dishwashing liquid into the notch. Put the surfboard back in the water and watch it go!

HOW DOES IT WORK?

The molecules that make up water have a force that makes them pull toward each other. On the surface they pull more strongly, creating surface tension. This makes it hard for small objects to break the surface, so they stay on top. Dishwashing liquid breaks up the surface tension, causing the water molecules (and the pepper and surfboard) to be drawn toward the unaffected water. This makes the pepper and the surfboard move.

ELASTIC TUB BOAT

This isn't a tugboat, it's a tub boat! It has a rotating paddle to push it forward, just like some real boats. Make two and have a race!

WHAT YOU'LL NEED:

* A clean, dry, plastic ice cream tub or margarine tub, with a lid
* Two popsicle sticks
* Heavy-duty tape or duct tape
* A rubber band, slightly longer than the width of the tub
* Scissors
* ⚠ ASK AN ADULT!

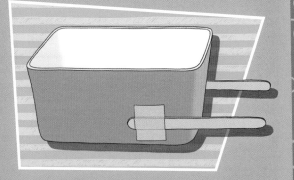

1. Use the tape to attach the sticks onto the tub, one on each side, just above the base. About half of each stick should stick out at one end, like this.

Another way to stick them on is to use a hot glue gun, but you'll need to ask an adult to do this for you.

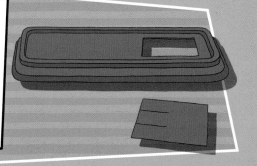

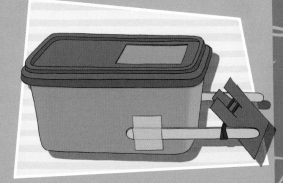

2. Now take the plastic lid, and ask an adult to cut a square out of it, about 2 x 2 inches (5 x 5 cm). Cut two slots, 1 inch (2.5 cm) apart, from one side of the square up to the middle.

3. Loop your rubber band around the ends of the two sticks. Then slot the plastic square onto one side of the rubber band, using the two cuts, to make a paddle.

4. Hold the boat and turn the paddle around and around so that it makes the rubber band twist. Keep going until the rubber band is tightly twisted.

5. Put the boat into calm water in a bathtub or paddling pool, and watch it go!

HOW DOES IT WORK?

As the rubber band gets twisted around and around, it gets stretched. This stores up a supply of energy. When you let the paddle go, the rubber band unstretches, which makes it unwind, using that stored energy to turn the paddle. Each time the paddle turns, it pushes against the water, making the boat move along.

EXPLODING ROCKET

Use the explosive power of a baking soda and vinegar reaction to send a rocket up, up, and away.

WHAT YOU'LL NEED:

* A small plastic tube-shaped container with a tight-fitting pop-off lid
* Craft cardboard
* Scissors
* Clear tape
* Felt-tip pens
* Baking soda (sometimes known as bicarbonate of soda)
* A teaspoon
* White vinegar
* A smooth, flat surface outdoors, with lots of space around it

⚠ ASK AN ADULT!

An old-style photographic film canister makes a perfect rocket. Vitamin tablets and beads often come in this kind of container, too.

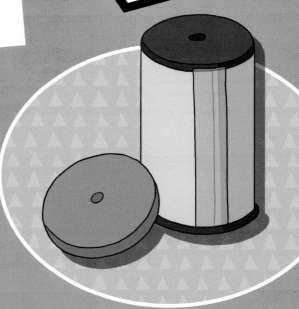

1. First, take the lid off your plastic tube, and roll a piece of cardboard around it to make a rocket shape. Tape it in place so that the open end of the tube is at the bottom.

2. Cut a circle of cardboard slightly wider than your rocket, then cut a slot in it from the side to the middle. Shape it into a nose cone for the rocket, and tape it on.

3. Cut cardboard triangles to make four rocket fins. Tape them onto the rocket at the base, to help it stand up. You can also draw on windows, numbers, or other details.

4. Turn the lid from the tube upside down, and carefully tip a teaspoon of baking soda into the middle. Turn the rocket over and half-fill the tube with vinegar.

Everyone should stand well back to watch the rocket take off. DON'T get too close or lean over it!

5. Ask an adult to quickly put the lid onto the tube, tipping the baking soda inside as they do so. They should press it on firmly, stand the rocket on the ground, and move away quickly!

HOW DOES IT WORK?
The vinegar and baking soda react to make bubbles of carbon dioxide gas. As more and more gas gets made, it presses hard against the inside of the container. Finally—if it works!—it pushes the lid off with a bang, and this pushes the rocket upward into the air.

AIR BLASTER

You can use forces to make cars, boats, and rockets go—but this is a bit different. The air blaster simply shoots air! It's completely safe, so you can aim it at many different objects.

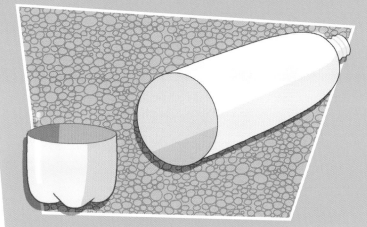

WHAT YOU'LL NEED:

* A large, plastic drink bottle
* A plastic bag, such as a sandwich bag
* Scissors
* A marker
* Strong clear tape or duct tape
* A strong rubber band

! ASK AN ADULT!

1. Ask an adult to cut the bottom end off the plastic bottle, as neatly as possible. Stand the bottle on the plastic bag, and draw a circle around it, about 1 inch (2.5 cm) bigger than the bottle on all sides.

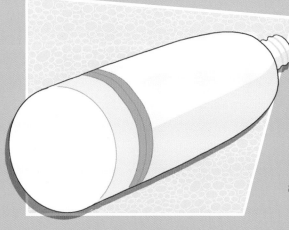

2. Carefully cut out the circle. Place the circle over the cut end of the bottle, and tape the edges to the bottle all the way around. Make the circle overlap the bottle by about ¼ inch (1 cm), so that the plastic is slightly loose.

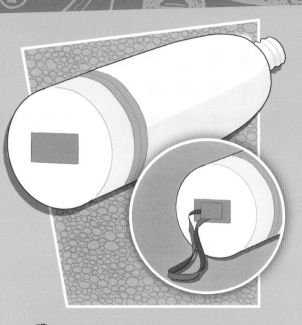

You can also use the air blaster to shoot at a target, such as a paper figure. Or ask an adult to light a candle, and see if you can use the blaster to blow it out from the other side of the room!

3. Stick a small piece of strong clear tape onto the middle of the plastic. Then use another piece to tape your rubber band onto the first piece to make a handle.

4. Now hold the bottle up and aim the open end at a target. Pull the rubber-band handle back, then let the handle go (keeping hold of the bottle while you do this). If you aimed right, a puff of air should hit your target—even if you're several yards away!

HOW DOES IT WORK?

When you pull the plastic back, you suck extra air into the bottle. When you let the rubber band go, the air is suddenly pushed out. But it has to get through the narrower neck of the bottle, and to do this it has to speed up. This creates a spinning, doughnut-shaped movement of air called a vortex, which can travel a long way in one direction.

GLOSSARY

centripetal force The force that draws a rotating object toward the center of rotation.

disposable Something that is intended to be thrown away after use.

electron A particle that is negatively charged.

energy The power to be active and perform jobs.

force An influence that often changes the motion of a body, or even causes a stationary body to move.

gravity A force that tries to pull two objects together. Earth's gravity is what keeps us on the ground, and what makes objects fall.

insulation The protection of an object from losing heat.

molecule A group of atoms that has bonded to form a chemical.

pressurized To place something under a force for a long period of time.

tension To be stretched tight as a result of forces acting against each other.

FURTHER INFORMATION

Books

Guinness World Records. *Science And Stuff*. London, UK: Guinness World Records Limited, 2018.

Mould, Steve. *How To Be A Scientist*. London, UK: DK Publishing, 2017.

Richards, Jon, and Ed Simkins. *Science In Infographics: Forces*. London, UK: Wayland Publishing, 2017.

Tatarsky, Daniel. *Cool Science Tricks: 50 Fantastic Feats for Kids Of All Ages!* London, UK: Portico, 2012.

Winston, Robert. *Home Lab: Exciting Experiments For Budding Scientists*. London, UK: DK Publishing, 2016.

Websites

http://www.sciencekids.co.nz/experiments.html
A whole host of experiments that let you explore the world of science.

https://www.stevespanglerscience.com/lab/experiments/ping-pong-popper/
These instructions will show you how to make a ping-pong popper!

https://www.exploratorium.edu/snacks/subject/mechanics
Discover over 40 science experiments that explore mechanics.

INDEX